You've
Been
Booed

It was just before Halloween
No costumes yet to be seen
Things we quiet and well
When I heard the door bell

I stood up and ran out to the door
And looked in the peep hole to see more
There was not a person in sight
And It gave me a bit of a fright.

I opened the door to see outside
There was nowhere for anything to hide
I looked to the left and to the right
But there was nothing in sight

What was sitting out of my door
Wasn't there before
The bag was closed on the top
But a note on the bag made me stop

She said the candy must have a history
And the note would help solve the mystery
So I looked up and tilted my head
And then this is the note my mom read.:

You've Been Booed!

The phantom ghost has come to town
To leave some goodies... I see you've found.
If you wish to make this a happier fall...
Continue this greeting, this phantom call.

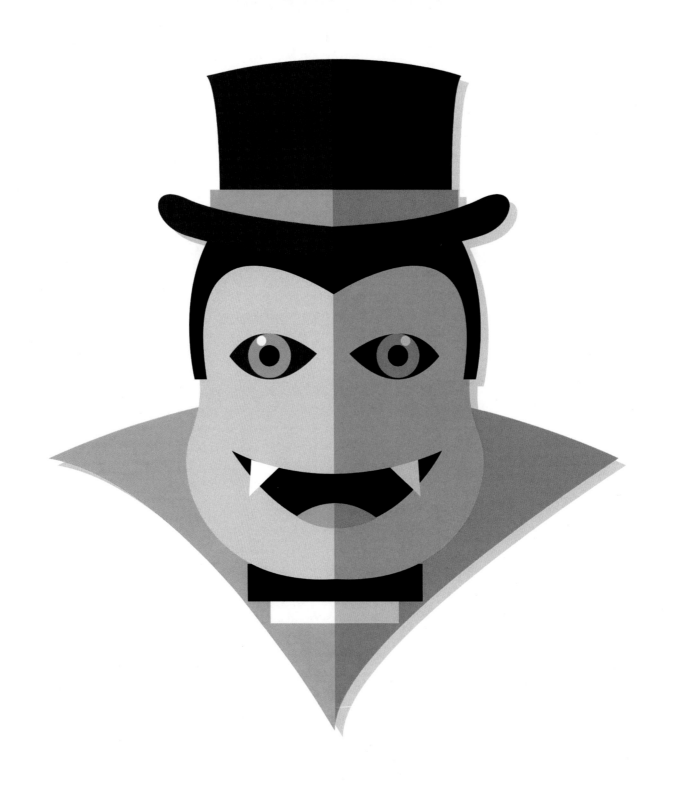

First, post this Phantom where it can be seen,
And leave it there until Halloween.
This will scare other Phantoms who may visit.
Be sure to participate, you don't want to miss it!

Second, make two treats & two copies from
www.beenbooed.com
Deliver them to two neighbors, try to stay calm.
Don't let them see you, be sneaky, no doubt
And make sure they put their Phantom Ghost out!

Next, you have only one day to act, so be quick!
Leave it at doors where the Phantom hasn't hit.
Deliver at dark when there isn't much light...
Ring the doorbell and run, and stay out of sight!!

And last, but not least, come join in the season.
Don't worry, be happy, you need no good reason.
This is all in good fun and we are just trying to say...
Happy Halloween & Have a Great Day!

Happy Halloween!

My mom smiled as she finished the note
Obviously happy with what the wrote
That night we ate the candy
Which I thought was just dandy

The next days she went to the store
So we could leave some treats at the door
We quietly delivered the treats to the door
We rang the doorbell and delivered more

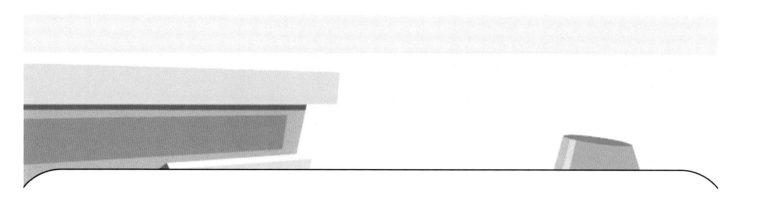

The phantom ghost has come to town
To leave some goodies... I see you've found.
If you wish to make this a happier fall...
Continue this greeting, this phantom call.

Happy Halloween

Made in the
USA
Columbia, SC